DREAMWORKS
HOW TO TRAIN YOUR
DRAGON
THE HIDDEN WORLD

MEET THE NEW DRAGONS

adapted by Maggie Testa
illustrated by Shane L. Johnson

SIMON SPOTLIGHT
An imprint of Simon & Schuster Children's Publishing Division • New York London Toronto Sydney New Delhi
1230 Avenue of the Americas, New York, New York 10020
This Simon Spotlight edition January 2019 • How to Train Your Dragon: The Hidden World © 2019 DreamWorks Animation LLC. All Rights Reserved.
All rights reserved, including the right of reproduction in whole or in part in any form. SIMON SPOTLIGHT and colophon are registered trademarks of Simon &
Schuster, Inc. For information about special discounts for bulk purchases, please contact Simon & Schuster Special Sales at 1-866-506-1949 or
business@simonandschuster.com. Manufactured in the United States of America 0219 LAK 10 9 8 7 6 5 4 3 2
ISBN 978-1-5344-3811-8 • ISBN 978-1-5344-3812-5 (eBook)

I am Hiccup Horrendous Haddock III, son of Stoick the Vast, and chief of Berk. Many years ago I did something no Viking had ever done before: I befriended a dragon . . . a Night Fury I named Toothless.

We Dragon Riders showed the other Vikings that dragons could be friends with humans. And so Berk became known as the world's first Dragon-Viking utopia—a place where dragons and Vikings could live peacefully together.

Soon other Vikings followed. My friend Astrid Hofferson learned to fly a Deadly Nadder she named Stormfly. Fishlegs Ingerman joined forces with a Gronckle dragon he named Meatlug. Snotlout Jorgenson paired up with a Monstrous Nightmare dragon called Hookfang. And the twins, Ruffnut and Tuffnut Thorston, began to ride the two-headed Hideous Zippleback known as Barf and Belch.

Since then the Vikings have discovered dozens of types of dragons from the tiny Terrible Terror to the massive Bewilderbeast . . . and learned all about their powers and personalities. After many years of study and training, the Vikings thought they had seen every kind of dragon, but they didn't know that more were out there. . . .

Recently we learned of the Crimson Goregutter and the Hobgobbler. We Dragon Riders first met these new dragons on a mission to rescue dragons from trappers. Trappers are people who still live in the old world, the one from before I proved that dragons and humans could—and should—be friends.

There are some people out there even worse than the trappers . . . hunters like Grimmel who live for the thrill of the hunt, especially of rare dragons like the Night Fury. But Grimmel cannot do this without the help of another type of dragon that the Vikings of Berk had never seen before . . .

the Deathgripper. Deathgrippers are armored dragons with bloodred underbellies and pincers instead of front legs. They also have venom: A small dose of a Deathgripper's venom will make a dragon calm and obedient, and a larger dose can kill a dragon.

Grimmel's plan was to capture Toothless and deliver him to greedy warlords who wanted to build a dragon army. If they had Toothless, the Alpha dragon, all other dragons would follow.

So Grimmel planted a trap on Berk in the form of a beautiful dragon controlled by a small dose of Deathgripper venom. Toothless found her in the woods and carefully approached to help her. She warned him of a nearby trap, and the two were instantly connected.

Toothless wanted to know more about the mysterious new dragon. Astrid named her Light Fury because she looked like a Night Fury but with white scales. She is just as fast and nimble as Toothless and as hard to see in the night sky. But the Light Fury can also camouflage herself in the daytime sky. In fact she can cause her scales to become mirrorlike, reflecting what's around her. Whenever she wants to, the Light Fury can appear almost completely invisible!

When Grimmel found Berk, I knew that the Vikings and dragons had to leave. It wasn't safe to stay anymore. My father had told me about a legendary place far away where dragons could be safe—a Hidden World. With Toothless leading the way for the dragons and Vikings of Berk, we set off to find it.

We soon discovered that someone was following us—the Light Fury! She knew the way to the Hidden World of dragons, and she wanted to take Toothless there. But Toothless had to go alone. I made a new tail fin for Toothless so he could fly free of his harness, without my help.

Not long after, Toothless caught up to the Light Fury and she took him to her home in the Hidden World. It was vastly different from anything Toothless had ever seen. It was the perfect place for the dragons of Berk—and all dragons—to live in safety, far away from those who would harm them. But it also meant that the Vikings and dragons of Berk had to say goodbye . . . possibly forever.

Years later we found out that Toothless and the Light Fury had babies called Night Lights! And as far as we know, the dragons still live peacefully and freely in the Hidden World.

Legend says that when the ground quakes or lava spews from the earth, it's the dragons letting us know they're still here, waiting for us to figure out how to get along. The world believes the dragons are gone . . . if they ever existed at all. But Berkians know otherwise, and we'll guard the secret until the time comes when dragons can return in peace.